THE
ABC
BUNNY

This special edition is published by arrangement with the
publisher of the regular edition, Coward-McCann, Inc.

CADMUS BOOKS
E. M. HALE AND COMPANY
Eau Claire, Wisconsin

TO GARY

A

for Apple, big and red

B

for Bunny snug a-bed

C for Crash!

D for Dash!

E

for Elsewhere in a flash

F

for Frog – he's fat and funny

"Looks like rain," says he to Bunny

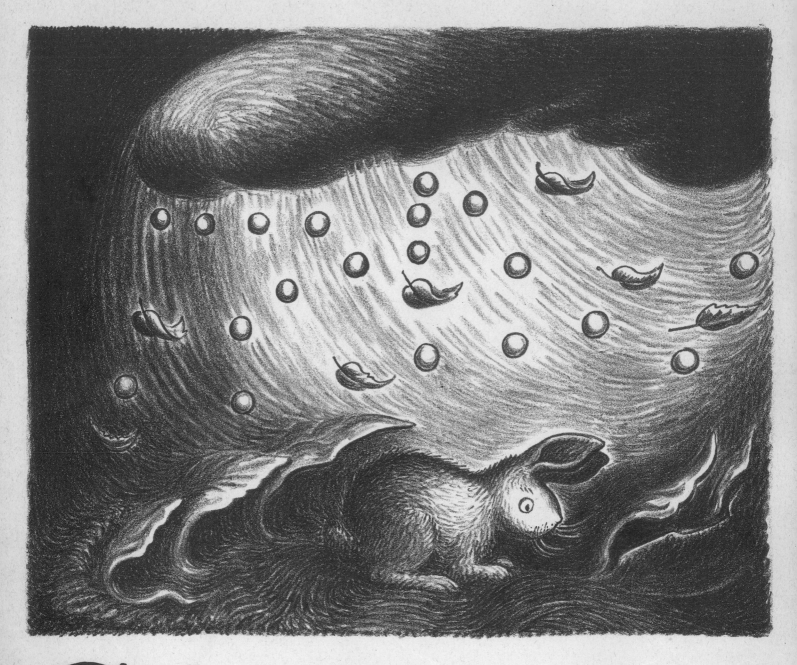

G for Gale!

H for Hail!

Hippy-hop goes Bunny's tail

K

for Kitten , catnip-crazy

L

for Lizard – look how lazy

M

for Mealtime – munch , munch , munch !

M-m-m! these greens are good for lunch

N

for Napping in a Nook

O

for Owl with bookish look

P

for prickly Porcupine

Pins and needles on his spine

Q for Quail

R for Rail

S

for Squirrel Swishy-tail

T

for Tripping back to Town

U

for Up and Up-side-down

V for View

Valley too

W

—"We welcome you!"

X

for eXit – off, away!

That's enough for us today

Y

for You , take one last look

Z

for Zero — close the book!

The illustrations in this book are original lithographs drawn by Wanda Gág. Printed in lithography by George C. Miller, New York, on paper made especially for this edition